OLD
TOM'S
Guide to Being Good

THIS BOOK BELONGS TO...

OLD TOM'S

Guide to Being Good

Written and Illustrated by

Leigh Hobbs

HAPPY CAT BOOKS

For Erica Irving & Dmetri Kakmi

Published by
Happy Cat Books
An imprint of Catnip Publishing Ltd
Islington Business Centre
3-5 Islington High Street
London N1 9LQ

First published by Penguin Books, Australia, 1998

This edition first published 2006
1 3 5 7 9 10 8 6 4 2

Text copyright © Leigh Hobbs, 1998
Illustrations copyright © Leigh Hobbs, 1998
The moral rights of the author/illustrator have been asserted

ISBN 10: 1 905117 12 4
ISBN 13: 978-1-905117-12-3

Printed in Poland

www.catnippublishing.co.uk

'I'm tired of the same old faces at my garden parties,' said the Queen with a sigh.

'Why not pick a name from the telephone book, Your Majesty?' suggested Sir Tassel Windburn, her able secretary.

'Splendid,' said the Queen.
Soon the royal finger stopped at a surname
beginning with 'T'.

And so, when Old Tom went to collect the mail one day,

there was a fancy looking letter, for Angela Throgmorton.

She was enjoying a well-earned rest, having cleaned the house from top to bottom.

But this was a letter that couldn't wait.
A royal invitation for two, for afternoon tea.

Angela knew the Queen was fussy about
good manners. So she dressed up and
wrote back straight away.

Angela had done her best to bring Old Tom up nicely.

He often happily helped around the house,

and sometimes did two chores at once.

But now that he was to meet the Queen,

Old Tom needed extra instruction in how to be good.

Angela invited a friend for tea.
'Pretend it's the Queen and practise your
manners,' she said.

Old Tom had learnt from his lessons that a nice smile is always handy.

He was eager to please and keen to be good.

So, when Angela's guest felt a little unwell,
kind Old Tom kept an eye on her.

Meanwhile, Angela went on with her eating instructions. 'If offered cake,' she said, 'say yes, please, and thank you, and don't drop your crumbs.'

There was a lot to remember, but Old Tom
was pleased with his progress.

Though Angela felt there was still work to
be done.

In fact, Angela was desperate.

But time had run out and Old Tom was as
good as he was going to get.

So Angela and Old Tom packed their bags
and off they went.

Angela was excited . . .

...and so was Old Tom.

After his journey, Old Tom was tired.

'I've never seen anything like this before,'
said the passport man.

At the hotel,

Angela explained that she was on a royal visit.

Then, in the evening, Old Tom and Angela practised their curtsies and bows.

Angela put on some gloves and pretended
to be the Queen.

'Kiss my hand,' she said.

In the morning, Angela got up bright and early. Old Tom had to have a bath …

... and she was needed to remove difficult
oily patches.

This was a big day, and Old Tom planned to look especially beautiful.

So, all morning, he combed and brushed
and fussed and even had his nails done.

When the arrival of lunch stopped him
cleaning his teeth,

he still remembered his manners, and gave
a big smile.

Luckily, Old Tom's good looks hadn't gone to his head.

Angela, too, had spent hours getting ready.
Now it was time for afternoon tea.

So Old Tom and Angela caught a bus to the palace.

When they arrived, Angela whispered,
'Now, remember your lessons and you'll
blend in quite nicely.'

Angela had expected only three for tea.
But she was polite and hid her disappointment.

Old Tom was on his best behaviour,

while Angela began to introduce herself
and make polite conversation.

'Angela Throgmorton's my name,' she said,
'and I'm here to meet the Queen.'

'Aren't we all?' replied Sir Cecil Snootypants.

At first, Old Tom was a little shy.

But soon he relaxed and made himself comfortable.

Angela kept an eye on things and whispered
helpful hints when no one was looking.

Old Tom remembered to look people
straight in the eye and make them feel special.

Then he had a rest from being good and made himself a sandwich.

Being good had certainly improved
his appetite.

Old Tom made friends quickly and even
found a favourite.

He was careful, of course, to leave room
for dessert.

Meanwhile, Angela was having a lovely time.

'What an unusual hat!' mumbled Boswell Croswell.

'I'm glad you like it,' was her gracious reply.

The afternoon-tea party was now in full swing.

'I hear the Queen has been delayed,'
said Lady Arabella Volcano to her
husband Horace.

While chatting to Sir Basil Bossy and his charming wife Babette, Angela noticed that Old Tom had gone.

She excused herself and began to search.
Angela tried to tempt Old Tom out with a
fresh chicken leg.

Angela described Old Tom to everyone
she met.

'Oh, my goodness!' cried Sir Bertie Boodle.

'Good gracious!' shrieked Lady Winifred
Pineapple De Groote and her husband
Sir Ernest.

'It can't be human!' cried Clarissa Cul-de-Sac just before she fainted.

Angela had mislaid
Old Tom, and wanted
him back before the
royal host arrived.

'By the way, where *is* the Queen?' asked Sir
Dalvin Dooper.

Suddenly there was silence, apart from a tiny shriek from Lady Pineapple.

Her Majesty had arrived at last …

... and she had company.

Angela was thrilled to see Old Tom and
nearly forgot her manners.

But not for long, of course.

'So you are my *other* special guest! I've
already met Old Tom,' said the Queen.
'And what jolly fun we've had!'

Her Majesty insisted that they stay the night.

After dinner there was a royal tour.
'That's my throne,' said the Queen.
And then it was time for bed.

The comfort of her guests was most
important. So that ...

...at breakfast, even if the Queen *had* seen Old Tom's little mistake, she was too polite to comment.

Goodbye!

Soon it was time to say goodbye.
The Queen had her royal duties and
Angela had work to do around the house.

As for Old Tom, he was happy with a kiss
from Angela, his guide to being good.

About Leigh Hobbs

Leigh Hobbs was born in Melbourne in 1953, but grew up in a country town called Bairnsdale.

Leigh wrote and illustrated *Horrible Harriet*, which was shortlisted for the 2002 Children's Book Council of Australia Book of the year Awards (Picture Books). As well as *Old Tom, Old Tom Goes to the Beach, Old Tom Goes to Mars, and Old Tom's Guide to Being Good* (Happy Cat Books), Leigh wrote and illustrated in full colour *Old Tom's Holiday* for Little Hare. His latest picture book is *Fiona the Pig*.

Leigh is also a sculptor and painter. He has a passion for English history and London is his favourite city, which he visits as often as possible.

Leigh has two dogs, a Blue Heeler and a Kelpie. He feels no affinity with cats, however, he may well admit to one exception …

www.leighhobbs.com

Read these books and join Old Tom on all his adventures

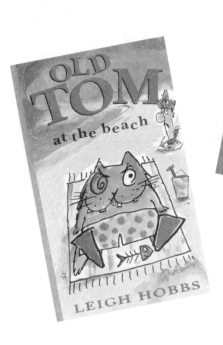

'Old Tom – a free spirit, at all times inquisitive, fearless and ready for action ... a bold and economical line captures every posture and gesture'

Books for Keeps